S0-BRF-509

Kouts Public Library
101 E. Daumer Road
Kouts, IN 46347

Moose

Porter County Public Library

Kouts Public Library
101 E. Daumer Road
Kouts, IN 46347

kjjnf   KO
599.657 LOHHA

Loh-Hagan, Virginia, author
Moose
33410014495834   08/18/17

Published in the United States of America by Cherry Lake Publishing
Ann Arbor, Michigan
www.cherrylakepublishing.com

Reading Adviser: Marla Conn MS, Ed., Literacy specialist, Read-Ability, Inc.
Book Design: Jennifer Wahi
Illustrator: Jeff Bane

Photo Credits: © Chase Dekker / Shutterstock.com, 5; © Images by Dr. Alan Lipkin / Shutterstock.com, 7; © Coprid / Shutterstock.com, 9; © Steve Boice / Shutterstock.com, 11; © Josef Pittner / Shutterstock.com, 13; © Thomas Aberg Lionstyle / Shutterstock.com, 15; © Tom Tietz / Shutterstock.com, 17; © Olenyok / Shutterstock.com, © C_Gara / Shutterstock.com, 21; © Greg and Jan Ritchie / Shutterstock.com, 23; © Ozerina Anna 2-3, 24; Cover, 1, 6, 16, 20, Jeff Bane

Copyright ©2018 by Cherry Lake Publishing
All rights reserved. No part of this book may be reproduced or utilized in
any form or by any means without written permission from the publisher.

Library of Congress Cataloging-in-Publication Data has been filed and is available at catalog.loc.gov

Printed in the United States of America
Corporate Graphics

table of contents

About the author: Dr. Virginia Loh-Hagan is an author, university professor, former classroom teacher, and curriculum designer. She learned that moose is an Alonquian word meaning "twig-eater." She lives in San Diego with her very tall husband and very naughty dogs. To learn more about her, visit www.virginialoh.com.

About the illustrator: Jeff Bane and his two business partners own a studio along the American River in Folsom, California, home of the 1849 Gold Rush. When Jeff's not sketching or illustrating for clients, he's either swimming or kayaking in the river to relax.

looks

Moose are large deer. They have big ears. They have long faces. They have **bells**. Bells are flaps of skin. They hang under moose's chins.

Moose have long, thin legs. They have sharp **hooves**. Their hooves are split. This lets them walk in snow and mud.

Male moose are called **bulls**. They have big **antlers**. They **shed** their antlers in winter. They grow new ones in spring.

Moose live in the north. They live in the United States and Canada. They live in forests. They live near water.

Moose like cold weather. They like snow. They have lots of **fur.** Their hair is **hollow**. This keeps them warm.

food

Moose eat a lot. They eat plants. They eat **twigs** and bark. They have special lips. Their lips move like fingers. This helps them grab food.

What plants do you eat?

Moose eat water plants. They are the only deer that eat underwater. They are good swimmers.

Moose like to be slow. They hang out in one place. But when they get mad or are afraid, they move. They run fast. They kick hard.

Moose are active at **dawn** and **dusk**. They spend a lot of time finding food. They like being alone.

Female moose are called **cows**. They have one or two babies a year. Moose live about 15 years.

glossary

antlers (ANT-lurz) branched horns made of bone

bells (BELZ) flaps of skin that sway from moose's throats

bulls (BULZ) name for male moose

cows (KOUZ) name for female moose

dawn (DAWN) the first appearance of light in the sky before sunrise

dusk (DUHSK) the time before night when it is not yet dark

fur (FUR) coat of hair that keeps an animal warm

hollow (HAH-loh) having a hole or empty space inside

hooves (HOOVZ) horny coverings on animals' feet

shed (SHED) to cast off, to lose

twigs (TWIGZ) small branches

index